For Jimmy and Galen, who always want to know how the pigs are doing.

Clarion Books
a Houghton Mifflin Company imprint
215 Park Avenue South, New York, NY 10003 • Copyright © 2001 by Eileen Christelow • The illustrations were executed in
watercolor and pen and India ink. • The text was set in 20-point BeoSans. • All rights reserved. • For information about permission
to reproduce selections from this book, write to Permissions, Houghton Mifflin Company, 215 Park Avenue South, New York, NY 10003.
www.houghtonmifflinbooks.com • Printed in the USA.

Library of Congress Cataloging-in-Publication Data
Christelow, Eileen • The great pig search / Eileen Christelow. • p. cm. • Summary: Bert and Ethel go to Florida to look for their runaway pigs and find
them in unexpected places. • ISBN 0-618-04910-X • [1. Pigs—Fiction. 2. Florida—Fiction.] I. Title. • PZ7.C4523 Gs 2001 • [E]—dc21 • 00-065560
WOZ 10 9 8 7 6 5 4 3 2 1

EILEEN CHRISTELOW

— THE —

Great Pig Search

CLARION BOOKS
New York

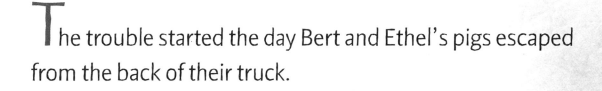

The trouble started the day Bert and Ethel's pigs escaped from the back of their truck.

Right after that, people all over town started missing clothes. Everyone searched everywhere.

No clothes. No pigs.

Bert grumbled for days. "I raised those pork chops from baby piglets! And what do they do? Hightail it out of here without so much as a thank-you!"

"Oh, cheer up!" said Ethel. "You aren't the first farmer to have pigs run away. If I were a pig, that's what I'd do. Beats being bacon any day."

HOME
SWEET
HOME

4

Well, Bert might have forgotten about those pigs except for a postcard that arrived a few weeks later. It was from a town in Florida.

"Who would send us a postcard that says 'OINK!'?" gasped Ethel.

"That should be obvious," said Bert.

Soon everyone in town was joking about Bert and his postcard-writing runaway pigs. There were stories in the newspaper, on the radio, and even on TV.

"This is embarrassing," grumbled Bert. "It's a humiliation."

"What we need is a vacation!" said Ethel. "It'll help you forget about those pigs."

So Bert bought two bus tickets . . . to Florida.

"Now, see here," said Ethel. "If we're going to Florida, I want to sit on the beach, dance under the stars, and go fishing. I do NOT want to look for pigs!"

"Don't worry," said Bert. "I won't even think about pigs. . . . But if I happen to see them, I'm bringing them home!"

Two days later, Bert and Ethel
arrived in Florida.

"See?" said Ethel. "No pigs."

8   "Don't be so sure," said Bert.

They took a taxi to their motel.

"We're looking for runaway pigs," Bert told the driver. "Have you seen any?"

The driver grunted loudly and drove through several red lights.

When they arrived at the Starlight Motel, the driver dropped off Bert and Ethel and left in a hurry.

"We are *not* looking for pigs!" said Ethel. "Remember?"

But when they checked into the motel, Bert told the desk clerk, "We'll be here for a few days. We're looking for runaway pigs. Have you seen any?"

The desk clerk suddenly squealed. She tossed them their room key and vanished.

"Stop asking about pigs," hissed Ethel. "People will think you're strange!"

12

As soon as they had unpacked, Bert and Ethel went for a walk. Bert asked everyone they passed, "Seen any runaway pigs?"

"NO PIGS," they all said.

"Bert!" warned Ethel. "Forget about the pigs!"

Bert and Ethel went to the beach and waded in the surf.
Bert tried to forget about pigs.

"Isn't this the life?" asked Ethel. "Salt air, cool breezes . . ."

" . . . but no pigs," Bert grumbled to himself.

That night, back at the motel, Bert and Ethel were almost
asleep when they heard a strange squealing sound.

"Sounds like the air conditioner is about
to break," said Ethel.

"Sounds like pigs!" said Bert.
He got up to look.
NO PIGS.

The next morning Bert and Ethel were headed out to breakfast when the desk clerk handed them a map.

"Directions to where we might find pigs!" gasped Bert.

"But I don't want to find pigs," said Ethel. "We're on a vacation! Not a pig hunt!"

"It'll be an adventure," said Bert. "We'll see the sights."

"This had better be good," said Ethel.

So they set out.

It was a long, prickly, sticky, hot walk.

There were NO PIGS.

But there was plenty of adventure!

"That desk clerk doesn't know anything about pigs!"
groaned Bert.

"If we get out of here alive, I'm going home,"
muttered Ethel.

Bert and Ethel didn't get down from the tree and back to the motel until late that afternoon.

Ethel started to pack her suitcase.

"You just won't forget about those pigs!" she shouted. "So I'm going home!"

Bert had a hard time convincing her to stay.

That evening, Bert took Ethel to a fancy restaurant.
"Turnip tarts!" said Ethel. "My favorite!"
"No pork chops?" Bert grumbled. "No sausage? No ham? What can I eat?"
"Bert!" warned Ethel. "NO PIGS! You promised!"

After dinner, Bert took Ethel dancing.
"This makes up for a bad day!" said Ethel, as they
rocked and rolled to the music of the Squealers.
But then Bert thought he saw . . .

"A PIG!" he shouted.

There was pushing and shoving and squealing and yelling as Bert raced across the dance floor.

"Bert!" shrieked Ethel. "No! Stop! That's not—" But it was too late.

Bert was hauled down to the police station for creating
a disturbance. He had a difficult time explaining about
runaway pigs.

Finally, the sergeant said, "I'm going to let you go, but
believe me, there are NO PIGS wandering around this town!"

The next morning, Bert and Ethel hired a boat and went fishing.

"Don't even bother looking for pigs out here!" snapped Ethel.

But Bert wasn't thinking about pigs. He felt much too seasick.

Suddenly, he felt something tug on his line.
"Hold on!" shouted the captain. "It's a big one!"
Bert braced himself and gripped his fishing rod.
The boat hit a big wave. Bert pitched out of his
seat . . .

27

"MAN OVERBOARD!"

"LET GO OF THE ROD!" screamed Ethel.

But Bert held on.

28

If it hadn't been for the bravery of one member of the crew, Bert might have drowned.

Back on shore, the story was already out.
The newspapers all wanted a picture of the
fellow who wouldn't let the fish get away.

Bert sighed happily. "Folks back home won't
joke about *this* story!"

The next morning, Bert and Ethel and the fish (packed in dry ice) headed home. Just before the bus left, Ethel hurried to the newsstand to buy the morning paper.

Bert and his fish were front-page news. There was even a photo of the fisherman who had rescued Bert.

"Oh, no!" gasped Ethel. "Who would believe it!"

Ethel didn't show Bert that newspaper until they were almost home.